TWO SIDES

For Alexa – Polly

To my Archie and Bella, the best of friends – Binny

First American Edition 2019
Kane Miller, A Division of EDC Publishing

Text copyright © Polly Ho-Yen, 2019
Illustrations copyright © Binny Talib, 2019

First published in Great Britain in 2019 by Stripes Publishing Ltd,
an imprint of the Little Tiger Group.

For information contact:
Kane Miller, A Division of EDC Publishing
P.O. Box 470663
Tulsa, OK 74147-0663

www.kanemiller.com
www.edcpub.com
www.usbornebooksandmore.com

Library of Congress Control Number: 2018958209

Printed and bound in China
STP/1800/0243/0419

2 4 6 8 10 9 7 5 3 1

ISBN: 978-1-61067-899-5

TWO SIDES

I'm Lula.

And I'm Lenka!

Polly Ho-Yen & Binny Talib

Kane Miller
A DIVISION OF EDC PUBLISHING

The Day That Everything Goes Wrong
starts like any other.

I wake up very, VERY late.

Mom says I'm the only person in the world
who can sleep through an alarm clock going off,
Hen barking, and her shouting

"LULA! GET UP NOW!"
all at the same time.

I dress in a rush and don't even have time to make my bed, but I manage a few mouthfuls of toast and do one of the quickest toothbrushings in history.

And I make sure I wrap up the present I made for Lenka last night.

"Have a great day, Lula!" Mom yells as I hurtle through the front door.

"Byeeeeeee!"

I shout back. The door slams behind me. I have the feeling I've forgotten something, although I'm in too much of a hurry to figure out what it is.

I tear down the street toward Lenka's house.
Like I said, it starts like any other day.

As usual, Lula is late. Suddenly there's a
TAP-TAP-TAP on the window.

Then a loud whisper:

"Lenka!
It's meeeeeee!"

I sling my schoolbag over my
shoulder and whisper goodbye to
Mom, who kisses me on the head.
I tiptoe out. We have to be quiet
in the mornings. My dad has to
sleep because he works nights.

Lula paces by the gate.
"Hello, 'me,'" I say.

"Come on!" Lula cries.
"We're going to be late!"

"You always say that.
Why don't you come by a bit earlier?
Then we wouldn't have to rush."

"You don't have to wait
for me, you know."

"I know I don't have to," I say.
"But if I didn't … then…"

"…we wouldn't be able
to go together,"
Lula grins.

We almost miss the bus, but some
of the other children see us
running and make the driver wait.

I wonder now how different things
might be if we had missed it.

It might have been a day like any other.

11

There might be another version of us going around – a Lula and Lenka that stayed just the same:

best

friends

forever.

Lula's been my best friend forever.

People say that a lot –

best friends forever

– but for us it's actually true.

We were born on the very same day.
Our moms met because they were
in the hospital together when they were
waiting for us to be born.

From when we were the smallest of
babies, we have always known each other.

The only time we're apart is when I go
away to see my grandma, but then I write
to Lula instead and send her drawings.

It's almost as good.

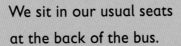

We sit in our usual seats
at the back of the bus.

Lenka likes to look out
of the window, but I like
to talk...

...and so we spend
the journey doing
half and half.

Although we've been
friends for our whole lives,
sometimes people say that we're
like chalk and cheese.

Or pens and peanuts.
Or penguins and pencils.
Or any two things that are quite
different from each other.

21

Summer is my favorite time of the year,
but Lenka prefers it when it's very cold,
and the sky is completely white.

Lenka doesn't really like Hen.
She's more of a Cat Person, but I think
he's the best creature in the world.

And I'm really messy. Sometimes you can't even see the floor of my bedroom because there's stuff piled up all over it. But Lenka is super tidy. She *always* puts things away and makes her bed in the morning.

Lenka prefers bare trees – she
says she likes the shape of the
branches with no leaves on them.
But I like trees green and shady.

It's never mattered though –
us being different – because…

...we're **best friends.**

Mom said it was a good thing because it made me think about things in a new way.

She's right, because when I look at them carefully I can almost understand why Lenka thinks branches with no leaves can look beautiful. And sometimes I meet a cat that's not unfriendly, and I think that I rather like them, too.

After Lula tells me about how her dog, Hen, ate a light bulb the night before, we fall into silence, and I look out of the window.

I like spotting people I can draw. I try to take a photo of them in my mind, and then when I can, I try to draw them.

Lula's the only one who knows I do this. Sometimes she even points out to me someone she thinks I might like to draw.

Lula much prefers talking to people.
She could walk up to just about anyone
and start a conversation. I like watching
people. I don't really like talking to anyone
that I don't know.

"What about that lady?" I point out an old woman wearing a huge fur hat that almost dwarfs her face.

Lenka looks over and stares at her carefully until she becomes tiny in the distance.

I suddenly remember the present that I made
for Lenka and reach down to my bag to find it.

My bag is full of things that shouldn't be in there
— pencil shavings, two old brown tangerines,
the remote control for the television.

Finally my hand closes around

the present.

Lula starts rummaging through her bag.

"Ah, my pencil case!"

I say as I see her searching.

"I'm glad you remembered."

Yesterday I lent Lula my coloring pencils.
I didn't really want to, if I'm honest
– I was working on a drawing for the art
competition at the library – but Lula said
she really needed them.

"The deadline for the competition is today,"
I tell her. "I just need to do some finishing
touches, and then I can hand it in after school."

"Your pencil case!" I shriek.
"I'm so sorry – I left it at home.
I knew I'd forgotten something."

"But you promised…"

Lenka turns away quickly so
I can't see her face.

"I put it on the end of my bed,
but it must have fallen off.
I was in such a rush this morning…"

"Why didn't you put it in your bag?
Or get up on time?"

Lenka's voice sounds odd: both quiet
and squeaky at the same time.

"I'm sorry," I say. "Do you think you
could use the pencils at school
to finish it?"

"The school's pencils aren't
in the right colors…"
Lenka says, still staring
out of the window.

"Maybe someone else has ones
you could borrow," I suggest.
I hold out the present toward her.
It was the whole reason why
I needed to borrow her pencils.

"Look, why don't you open your present? I made it for you last night."

I can't help but glance over. It's
wrapped in Lula's usual style – a piece
of wrapping paper that isn't quite big
enough, with newspaper covering the rest.

For a moment, I want to forget that
Lula didn't bring my pencil case.
I want to forget the hot, itching feeling
that's building behind my eyes. But then
she says,

"Honestly, don't worry about your drawing –
if you turn it in just as it is I know it will still
win. It's brilliant already!"

A wave of anger surges up inside me.
I shout:

"I don't want
your present!
I want my pencil case.
It's not that difficult
to understand,
is it?"

For a moment I can't even open my mouth to speak, I'm so stunned.

"I didn't do it on purpose," I say in the end.

"You knew it was important to me," Lenka shouts, "but you just didn't bother to make the effort because it wasn't important to you. You only ever think of yourself."

"Well if that's the way you feel, then maybe we shouldn't be friends," I say, without thinking. I feel stung.

"Fine by me."

"Fine," I say. I stuff the present back into my bag and go and sit as far away from Lenka as I can.

My breath comes in ragged bursts.
I have to clamp my lips together
to try and stop myself from crying.
But one tear trails down my cheek.
I turn my head so no one can see it.

Lula sits at the front of the bus.
I bite my lip to try to stop the tears
which I can feel building behind
my eyes.

I turn away to the window again.
I can see my reflection in it.

A tear rolls silently down my cheek.

The day after The Day
That Everything Goes
Wrong, I am already up
and dressed when Mom
comes in to wake me.

"This is a first, Lula!"
she says. "Are you
feeling better, then?"

I'd told Mom that
I wasn't feeling well
when I got home from
school yesterday, and
she'd believed me.

She tucked me up in
bed and brought me
dinner on a tray.
I didn't tell her what
happened with Lenka.

Hen seemed to know
though. He's barely
left my side since
I got home and won't
stop licking my face.

I have time to eat
what Mom calls "a
proper breakfast" and
even brush my hair
and my teeth before
I need to leave.

As I pass by Lenka's house, I quickly
push her pencil case through the
mail slot and speed away.

For the first time ever, I have to wait for a while before the bus comes, all by myself. Without Lenka, I feel like I stick out to everyone.

When I tell Mom that I have a pain in my stomach she says that I can stay at home. I'm not lying, I do feel a pain there
– although I know it's not because I'm ill.

I watch Lula walk up the street. She stops when she gets to our house.

My ears strain for her knock, but there's a different sound instead – something being shoved through our mail slot. I run down the stairs to see what it is.

My pencil case.

I think that there might be a note,
but there's nothing with it.

I tuck it into my schoolbag and then
pull out my unfinished drawing for
the library competition. I decided
not to hand it in. Instead I scrunch
it up and toss it into the trash can.

Afterward I wrap myself tightly in my duvet and make a ball with my body. Dad says that I look like a hedgehog when he comes to see me.

I think that I actually AM a little bit like one: I feel prickly, and I want to hide so that no one can see my face.

School feels like a different
place without Lenka.

I keep spotting things that I think she
would like and turn to tell her before
I remember that she's not there.

I try to talk to other people.

But when I open my mouth, I start
telling them about the shapes the
bare branches of the trees make...

Soon it becomes clear they don't
understand what I mean.

It's very quiet in my bedroom.

I try to draw, but the pictures keep going wrong.

The next morning, I make sure that I'm out of the house early. On the bus, I sit as far away as I can from where IT happened.

When Lula gets on she sits

as

far away

from me

as

she can.

As soon as I get into class, I see that
Lenka is sitting as far away from where
we usually sit together as she can.

I try not to look at the empty seat
beside me.

On our way to the library, our
class stops at the playground.

Our teacher, Miss Randall,
says: "Go play!"

I don't feel like playing.

I head for the swings because there
are only a few people over there,
but when I get close, I realize that
Lula is on one of them.

I **kick** my swing off hard and soar high into the air.

I pretend that she's not there,
although she's really close to me.
I try to make my swing go so high
that it makes me feel dizzy.

When Lenka runs over to the swings,
I think at first that she is coming to tell
me that she is sorry.

I stop swinging … but she just jumps
onto the empty swing next to me
and flies off from the ground.

The words I was going to say, I whisper
to myself…

"I'm sorry, too."

They float away in the wind. No one
hears them.

I tell myself that we are too different
after all, and that I have to make new
friends. I have to forget all about her.

Lula sits with other people in the classroom.

And plays with other people on the playground.

And eats with other people at lunchtime.

I sit and play and eat by myself.

It gives me more time, I tell myself, to think about other things, like drawing. But I'm still finding it hard to make my pictures go right.

I feel very tight on the inside. I don't know what to do to make the feeling go away.

My new best friend is called Maya.

She likes to talk almost as much as I do.

She speaks with such a **big voice**

that I have to talk with an *even*

bigger voice so she can hear me.

We keep getting into trouble in class for talking too loudly. Miss Randall says if I carry on like this then she and I will need to talk about my behavior.

My mom asks me why Lula has
stopped coming around.

I don't want to tell her. But she
keeps asking me over and over,
and so I tell her the truth.

"She's not my friend anymore,"

I say.

"She's not my friend anymore," I tell
Miss Randall when she asks me why
I'm not talking to Lenka.

"I see," she says, but she looks worried
and glances over to where Lenka is.
She's kneeling in the corner of the
playground looking at something on
the ground.

She's all alone. She hasn't made
any other friends.

"Did something happen?" Miss Randall asks. "Have you tried talking to her about it?"

But at that moment, a boy hobbles over to us, clasping his knee and crying. While Miss Randall deals with him, Maya runs over and tells me that I need to pretend that I am a horse for a game.

Maya always tells me what she wants me to do when we play together.

Although I used to try and tell her what I wanted, I've found it's easier if I just go along with her.

I can't help wondering what it would be like to be something as small as an ant.

I imagine it would be quite scary.

Almost everything is bigger than you.

And no one would care if they stood on you – they probably wouldn't even notice.

But I also know that ants do amazing things. They can move objects much bigger than themselves and make anthills when they all work together.

"Out of the way! Coming through!"

calls a voice.

A girl from one of the younger years almost runs into me. She bounds toward a brownish loop of a jump rope lying on the playground behind me.

Maya is galloping around the edge
of the playground, flaring her nostrils
and not looking where she's going.

She almost runs straight into a
younger girl who is determinedly
running toward something.

I follow the girl's gaze. There's a
jump rope lying on the ground,
but just as she gets to it,
Maya darts toward it.

They both lunge for the rope.

At the very moment the younger girl reaches for the snake of rope, Maya grabs for it, too. They both pull at the rope and unfurl it until it's stretched out to its full length.

73

"I was here first!"

they say at exactly the same time.
Neither of them will let go.
They say it again, together:

"I was here first!"

I run over to them. They have both
started to cry fat raindrop tears.

I spot Lenka running toward them, too.

"Don't cry," I say, although this only
makes them howl a little louder.

Then Lula's next to me.

"Hey! You two!" she shouts. They look at her, stunned. "There's no point getting so upset over a … over a … jump rope!"

"But I saw it first," Maya says.

"No, I did!" the younger girl says.

"You both saw it at the same time actually," I say.

"Yes," Lula says. "It's both of yours – which means you are very lucky because you can play together."

"That's right," I say. "Playing with a friend is a million times better than playing by yourself."

I look over to Lenka then.

"I'm so sorry I forgot to bring your pencil ca—" But before I can finish speaking, Lenka interrupts.

"I'm so sorry that I said what I did – it
wasn't true – you always think of other
people. You're kind, and generous…
I just got angry…"

"You had every right to be – you needed
your pencil case to finish your drawing.
I'm so sorry."

"It's OK." As I speak the words, I know
that they are true. Everything IS OK.
"I know you didn't mean it."

And then I see the most wonderful thing:
a smile begins to creep over Lenka's face.

The girls holding the rope are looking
from Lenka to me and back again.
They've stopped crying now.

"How do we play together?"
the younger one asks.

Suddenly Lenka and I can't stop laughing.
Our laughter rings out.

It's the happiest sound in the world.

"We'll show you,"
I say.

Lenka takes one end of the
rope, and I take the other,
and we swing it so it makes
a large, high circle.

The girls run into the
swinging rope and jump
and laugh and skip.

It's the funniest thing: I'd been playing The Day That Everything Went Wrong over and over in my head, and it always made me upset, but now it just seems so…

Silly!

I can't believe that I fought with Lula over something so silly. We smile at each other, and all those days of not talking and feeling lonely fade away.

"From now on," I say as we swing the rope, "the most important thing is that we stick—"

But Lula finishes the sentence before I can…

"Together!"